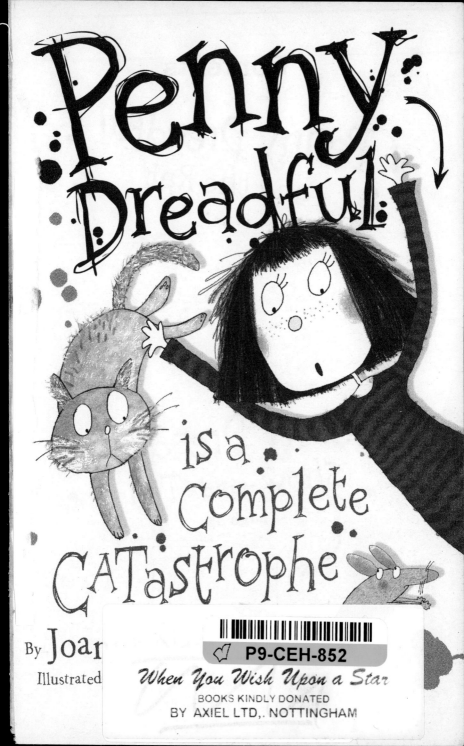

Penny Dreadful

is a Complete CATastrophe

By Joan

Illustrated

Contents

BIT OF
MOON
£100

Penny Dreadful
and the CATastrophe
page 95

Penny Dreadful's
Top 5 Tips for Survival
page 134

Meet Penny Dreadful and her Resigned Relations

Penny
(It's never really her fault...)

Cosmo
(Penny's best friend)

Georgia May Morton-Jones
(Penny's clever cousin)

Daisy
(Penny's annoying sister)

Penny's long-suffering **mum** and **dad**

Very prim-and-proper **Aunt Deedee**

Barry
(Miaow, I'm Gran's cat)

Gran
(Normally found fast asleep somewhere)

Penny Dreadful

and the
Rat

My name is not actually Penny Dreadful. It is Penelope Jones.

The "Dreadful" bit is my dad's **JOKE**. I know it is a joke because every time he says it he laughs like a honking goose. But I do not see the funny side.

Plus it is not even true that I am dreadful. It is like Gran says, i.e. that I am a **MAGNET FOR DISASTER**. Mum says if Gran kept a better eye on me in the first place instead of on *Paper Doily* in the three o'clock at Aintree then I might not be quite so magnetic. But Gran says if Mum wasn't so busy answering phones for Dr. Cement, who is her boss and who has bulgy eyes like hard-boiled eggs (which is why everyone calls him Dr. Bugeye), and Dad wasn't so busy solving crises at the council, then they would be able to solve some crises at 73 Rollins Road, i.e. our house. So you see it is completely not my fault.

✮ ✮ ✮ ✮

For instance, the **DISASTER** with Rooney, who is our class rat, might not have even been such a **DISASTER** if it wasn't for several many **OTHER** people, i.e.:

1. Georgia May Morton-Jones,

who is my cousin, and who should **NOT** have brought round her real leather briefcase with two compartments and a secret slot.

b. Lilya Bobylev, who is Georgia May Morton-Jones's au pair, and who should have taken an aspirin after all.

3. Cosmo Moon Webster, who is my best friend (even though he is a boy and exactly a week older than me), and who should not have made the **AMAZING MAZE**.

iv) Dad, who is my dad, who should not have claimed he was a **RESPONSIBLE ADULT**, because as Mum says, he is **CLEARLY NOT**.

e. Miss Patterson, who is our class teacher and very tall and thin like a beanpole, and who should have got a guinea pig after all.

But it **WAS** a **DISASTER**, and this is why…

✶ ✶ ✶ ✶

What happens is that Mr. Schumann, who is our headmaster, and who is mostly saying things like "Penelope Jones, for the umpteenth time will you please sit with your bottom on the chair and your feet on the floor and **NOT** the other way round", says something different, i.e. that our class is allowed a pet, and we will all take turns to look after it at weekends, and it will teach us about **RESPONSIBILITY**, and a guinea pig would be a good idea.

Only then Miss Patterson decides that the pet should teach us about **TOLERANCE** as well, i.e. we should get an animal that is **UNPOPULAR FOR NO GOOD REASON.** So then everyone starts to have **BRILLIANT IDEAS™** about what pet to get, e.g. Luke Bruce thinks we should get a shark and Cosmo thinks we should get a Tyrannosaurus rex. Only Miss Patterson says **a)** we cannot fit a shark into the classroom, and **b)** Tyrannosauruses are **EXTINCT** and **DEAD**.

So Bridget Grimes, who is top of the class and Mr. Schumann's favourite, says we should get a rat, because they are actually **CLEAN** and **CLEVER** (i.e. like her) and Miss Patterson agrees and the next day there is a rat in a glass tank where the locusts used to be (which is another story entirely). And then Miss Patterson says we can each put a name in a hat (only it is not a hat, it is an old paint pot), and she will pull one out and that is what we will call him, and it has to be a boy's name because it is a boy rat, so no *Princess*es please. So I put in *Ichabod* (which is

what my dad wanted to call me only Mum said no because it is too weird and also I am not a boy), and Cosmo puts in *Flame*.

Only Miss Patterson does not pull those names out she pulls out

ROONEY

which was Henry Potts's idea. So Cosmo gets cross because Henry Potts is his mortal enemy and he throws a rubber at him, and Henry throws a pencil tin back and it hits Rooney's glass tank and Rooney squeaks, and they both get sent to Mr. Schumann.

★ ☆ ★ ★

Mr. Schumann says their punishment is that they are **DISQUALIFIED** from looking after Rooney until they can learn some **RESPONSIBILITY**.

Only Cosmo says Rooney is supposed to be teaching them **RESPONSIBILITY**, so if they don't look after him how can they learn it? And Henry Potts agrees (even though he is a mortal enemy), and also says Mr. Schumann is being **INTOLERANT**.

Only Mr. Schumann does not agree and says

they will be disqualified for ever if they do not
PIPE DOWN. Which they do, and they decide
that Mr. Schumann is their mortal enemy for the
moment and they will not throw rubbers at each
other for at least an hour and a bit.

★ ★ ★ ★

So then
Miss Patterson
makes the rest
of us write our
own names
on pieces of
paper and put
those into the
hat that is
not a hat,

and she will pull one name out and that is who will get Rooney for the first weekend, and unbelievably it is **MY NAME**, i.e. Penelope Jones. And I can tell Bridget Grimes is not pleased about this, and nor is Miss Patterson, only she says maybe the **RESPONSIBILITY** will do me good.

And I think maybe **TOLERANCE** will do her good, but I do not say it because I do not want to get sent to Mr. Schumann and be **DISQUALIFIED**.

✦ ✧ ✦ ✦

Only when I get home on Friday with Rooney in the glass tank it is clear that Mum is not pleased either, because she says she is up to **HERE** with Barry (who is Gran's cat, and who has eaten the last of the cheese again, even though Mum has told Gran it is **CAT BISCUITS AND CAT BISCUITS ONLY**), and Daisy (who is my sister, and is very irritating, and who says she will die if she doesn't get a pony like Lucy B. Finnegan), and so the last thing she needs is more animal hoo-ha, especially with a filthy rat. So I tell her he is not filthy, he is in fact **CLEAN** and **CLEVER**,

and amazingly
Dad agrees
and he helps
me set up a
special maze for
Rooney with toilet
rolls and a cat
biscuit in the
middle, and
Rooney solves it
in thirty-three
seconds, which is
faster than Barry
(who just eats a
raisin he finds
on the floor).

And everyone agrees Rooney is a brilliant pet and **COMPLETELY CLEVER**, although Daisy says a pony would be **CLEANER** because ponies do not poo on your hand, which is true. And then I say it is time to put Rooney away because it is not just about **TOLERANCE** it is about **RESPONSIBILITY**.

And I prove I am utterly responsible because I do not let Rooney sleep in my bed that night, or investigate outside the window in the morning, or make friends with Barry, even though I have seen it on *Animal SOS* (which is a TV series where animals are always nearly dying but then they don't and it is **MIRACULOUS**), because Gran says Barry is not tolerant of anyone (e.g. the man who does the news), and so he is not likely to be friends with a rat, plus Barry is a brilliant hunter and will pounce on Rooney and murder him. So I responsibly keep Rooney in his glass tank in my bedroom and I feed him my cereal through the wire on the top, which is what we are doing when the doorbell goes.

It is my cousin Georgia May Morton-Jones,
with her au pair, Lilya Bobylev, who asks
Mum if she can look after Georgia May
because she has to see Dr. Cement about her
earache. Aunt Deedee, who is Georgia May's
mum and is usually shouting on the phone

to the **NEW YORK BOYS**, says pain is all in the mind and that when she broke her arm she only took an aspirin and did three conference calls and sacked Miss Fazakerley-Knowles before she went to hospital. Only Lilya says the pain is not all in her mind it is all in her ear. But Mum says she can't look after Georgia May because she has to see Dr. Cement, only not for earache, for filing, and Gran is not allowed to look after Georgia May except in **END OF THE WORLD EMERGENCIES** because of the time Georgia May shaved all her hair off. So Dad says **HE** will look after her, because he is a **RESPONSIBLE ADULT** and anyway, how hard can it be? And I can tell Mum is about to say something about that, and possibly so is Georgia May, but then the phone goes and it is Lucy B. Finnegan asking if Daisy can come horse riding, so then Mum has to find Daisy's jodhpurs and drop her off at the stables on the way to Dr. Cement's so it is agreed that Dad will be in charge.

Normally I am completely **GLOOMY** when Georgia May comes to play because she is only four and a bit, and not at all interested in my

BRILLIANT IDEAS™

in case they ruin her clothes or her fingers
(which are very important because
Mr. Nakamura says she shows potential
on the violin). Only this time I have Rooney,
and Georgia May is quite excited because she
has learned lots of interesting rat facts in
biological science at The Drabble Academy

for Girls,
e.g. that
rats see
with their
whiskers
and keep cool
with their tails.

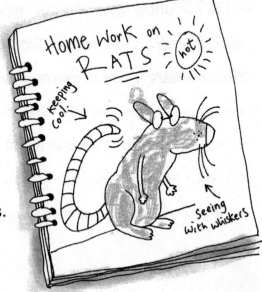

Home work on RATS   hot

keeping cool

Seeing
with whiskers

We do not have biological science at St Regina's, we have nature walks (only not at the moment because Miss Patterson says she is not taking anyone into Hooton Copse again until I can be trusted not to fall out of a tree). Anyway, we are about to test if Rooney can see with his whiskers, when it turns out that Mum was wrong because Dad is suddenly **VERY RESPONSIBLE** and says we are not allowed to let Rooney wander around the floor, in case of **UNFORESEEN CIRCUMSTANCES**, e.g. Barry. Only Georgia May says they are not **UNFORESEEN** because he has just **FORESEEN** them, but Dad says he is not getting into an argument about words, because in fact he could have

been a professor if he hadn't married Mum.
But Georgia May says no he could not,
because he does not have a real leather
briefcase, he has a pink rucksack with a
picture of a princess on it (which in fact he
borrowed from Daisy because Barry chewed
his black one). And Dad says it is not
essential to have a real leather briefcase to be
a professor and Georgia May says yes it is,
which is why Aunt Deedee bought her one
yesterday, and she shows it to him, and it is
very definitely real leather, plus it has two
compartments and a secret slot. Which is
when I have my

BRILLIANT IDEA™

which is to turn
her briefcase into
a portable rat
carrier, and we
can put Rooney
in the secret slot
and his food in
one of the
compartments
and his bed in
the other.

Only Georgia May Morton-Jones does not think this is so **BRILLIANT** because Rooney will poo on the leather, and Dad looks like he possibly agrees, only the doorbell goes again so he has to answer it. And this time it is Cosmo Moon Webster, who has come to be **RESPONSIBLE** and **TOLERANT** with Rooney too.

Then Dad has one of his

BRIGHT IDEAS™

(which are like **BRILLIANT** ones, only Mum almost never thinks they are **BRIGHT** or **BRILLIANT**), which is to make pizza for everyone for lunch. Only we don't have any cheese, because Barry has eaten it, so Dad says he will go to the shop and Gran can be in charge and it will only be for an hour and Aunt Deedee will never know.

✷ ✷ ✷ ✷

So for a while we are totally responsible, i.e. we watch *Animal SOS* with Gran (only Georgia May keeps her eyes shut because there is a monkey who miraculously **DOES NOT DIE** even though another monkey has bitten his arm and it is hanging off, and also because she is only allowed to watch the Maths Channel). But then Cosmo notices that Gran is fast asleep and says maybe it would be **RESPONSIBLE** to go upstairs and do something quiet, e.g. make Rooney a new and **IMPROVED** maze.

And we do, and it is an **AMAZING** maze,
because you start on the Pirate's Ship (which is
actually a shoebox with some sails),

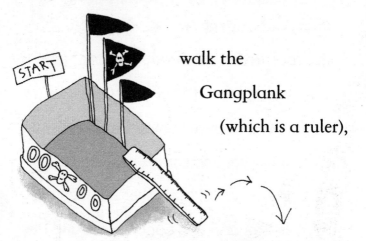

walk the

Gangplank

(which is a ruler),

dive into the

Shark-Infested Waters

(which is actually an old

biscuit tin with some plastic animals in),

then go through the Catacombs of Death

(which is fourteen toilet rolls joined up in a tube),

and into the Haunted
House (which is Daisy's
doll's house), up the
mini stairs, out the
mini bathroom window

and into the Prize Arena
(which is the glass tank), where there
is a chocolate digestive for a prize (because
for once Barry has eaten all the cat biscuits).

END

And Rooney is obviously as clever as a professor even without a real leather briefcase, because he goes along the Gangplank, into the Shark-Infested Waters – where he actually attacks a hammerhead (i.e. a plastic sheep) – then goes into the Catacombs of Death. Only the catacombs fall apart because Cosmo has trodden on them accidentally, and so I help Rooney a bit by putting him through the front door of the Haunted House.

And **THAT** is where the **DISASTER** begins, i.e. Rooney does not come out of the bathroom window. In fact he does not come out **AT ALL**.

So Cosmo says he has probably just decided to
have a sleep in the genuine oak miniature
four-poster bed with lace canopy. Only then
ten minutes have gone and he is still not awake,
and when we open up the front of the house the
genuine oak miniature four-poster bed only has
three posters left, and there is a big hole in the
wall, and Rooney is nowhere to be seen,

i.e. he is not in the
Catacombs
of Death, or
in the Pirate
Ship, or
even in my
bedroom.

So then Cosmo says maybe we should use Barry to sniff Rooney out, only we will capture Rooney with an ice-cream tub before Barry pounces and murders him. Only Barry is not too keen on getting up from the sofa because he is watching a programme about bees, so Cosmo gives him the chocolate digestive prize and he is keener all of a sudden.

And he does some sniffing
in my room and he finds
a lot of things, e.g.:

a) An old sock

2. A piece of liquorice

c. A dead fly

But **NO ROONEY**. Cosmo says he has probably
fled to his freedom, which is a **GOOD THING**,
because Cosmo's mum (who is called Sunflower,
even though her real name is Barbara) does not
believe in keeping animals locked in cages

because it is **AGAINST THEIR RIGHTS**. But I
do not think this is a **GOOD THING** and nor
will Miss Patterson and so I am suddenly very
gloomy, which is when Dad gets back with the
cheese and says, "Why the long face, Jones?"

And so I tell him, and amazingly instead
of telling me I am **IRRESPONSIBLE**, he says,

"He'll be in the plumbing. Rats always are."

And he gets a wrench and a pair of pliers,

and says,

> Did I ever tell you I could have been a plumber if I hadn't met your mother?

Only I do not think this is true because he
unscrews a bit of pipe and water bursts all
over everyone, which is when Mum and
Daisy and Lilya Bobylev
all walk in.

And then it is **MAYHEM** because Georgia May Morton-Jones is crying like **MAD** because she says she will catch a cold and will miss her violin exam and Mr. Nakamura will be disappointed in her,

and Lilya Bobylev is crying like **MAD** because Aunt Deedee will sack her for making Mr. Nakamura disappointed in Georgia May, and Daisy is crying like **MAD** because the wet has flooded her chewed-up doll's house. And she says,

It is **ALL YOUR FAULT**, Penelope Jones.

Only Mum (who has gone a bit palish and her lips are very thin), says it is not my fault, it is **DAD'S,** and he has proved that he is **NOT** a **RESPONSIBLE ADULT** and that it is the last time she is **EVER** leaving him in charge.

But even though she says it is not my fault I am still completely gloomy because I do not think Bridget Grimes or Miss Patterson or Mr. Schumann will agree when I go to school on Monday with no Rooney.

But then Dad has another of his

BRIGHT IDEAS™,

which is to go to Paradise Pets and buy a new rat that looks just like Rooney and **NO ONE WILL BE ANY THE WISER**. And Mum says this is really **NOT BRIGHT** because we are bound to get found out, only Dad does not agree and Mum says "Fine" because she has to sort out the pipes and Daisy's doll's house and some dry clothes for Georgia May Morton-Jones.

And so that is what we do. We buy a new rat called Rooney 2 and he looks just the same and so Dad is right – **NO ONE WILL BE ANY THE WISER**.

★ ★ ★ ★

Especially not Miss Patterson,
who is completely pleased
when I come in on Monday
with the glass tank and
Rooney 2 inside it, and
she says I have "proved
my critics wrong",
i.e. Bridget Grimes.

Only Bridget Grimes does not like being proved wrong, and in history, when we are supposed to be learning about King Alfred who burned some cakes, she is staring very hard at Rooney and says,

Miss Patterson, Miss, why is Rooney so fat? I think Penelope Jones has been feeding him irresponsible things and he is obese and will die.

Only for once Miss Patterson does not agree and reminds her about **INTOLERANCE** and makes her go and sit in the corner with Alexander Pringle, who is in trouble for eating peanut butter sandwiches in class again.

✶ ✦ ✶ ✦

And so I am just thinking that **DISASTER** has been **AVERTED** when it gets **VERTED** again, i.e. on Wednesday morning we go into class and Rooney has had eight rat babies. And I say it is a **MIRACLE** because Rooney is a boy.

Only Miss Patterson does not agree that it is **MIRACULOUS** and she sends me to Mr. Schumann, where I have to explain about the maze, and the pipes, and Rooney 2. But, like I tell him, it is not my fault, it is just that I am a **MAGNET FOR DISASTER**. Only Mr. Schumann does not agree and I am banned from learning about **RESPONSIBILITY** for the rest of the year, and so is anyone else until he can work out what to do with all the rat babies. So everyone else starts being very **INTOLERANT** because they do not get to look after Rooney 2 at all and Henry Potts says I have **IRRESPONSIBLY** lost Rooney 1 who has probably been eaten by **INTOLERANT** wolves or jaguars. And Cosmo says jaguars do not eat rats they eat boys called

Potts, and then Henry Potts says he is being **INTOLERANT**, and Cosmo says Henry is being **INTOLERANT** and then Miss Patterson tells everyone to stop the **INTOLERANCE NONSENSE** and open up their art books.

★ ☆ ✦ ✦

Only when I get home, I find out that I have not lost Rooney 1 and he has not been eaten by jaguars or wolves, he is back at Paradise Pets. What happened was he had been **ASLEEP** in the secret slot in Georgia May Morton-Jones's real leather briefcase. Only he woke up in her violin exam and bit Mr. Nakamura who was very **INTOLERANT** and failed Georgia May. And I know this because Aunt Deedee rings Mum to shout about the filthy rat.

But Mum tells Aunt
Deedee that in fact
rats are not filthy,
they are **CLEAN** and
CLEVER, and she
should be more
TOLERANT.

But Aunt Deedee says
there is such a thing as
TOO MUCH TOLERANCE,
which is why Georgia
May is on Grade 4
violin and I can't
even play "Twinkle
Twinkle Little Star" on the

recorder without getting several notes wrong.
So then Mum says something **INTOLERANT**
and **IRRESPONSIBLE** and Aunt Deedee puts
the phone down.

And I say in fact it is good that Mum
thinks rats are **CLEAN** and **CLEVER**,
because Mr. Schumann has actually had a
BRILLIANT IDEA™, which is that we can
take a rat baby to look after at home, but
only if we get **PERMISSION IN WRITING**. Only
Mum says she is up to here with rat nonsense,
and even if they could use the toilet and wash
their hands she is not giving
me **PERMISSION**
IN WRITING to
have a rat baby.

Daisy says, "It *is* all your fault, Penelope Jones, you are such a complete moron." But it is not my fault. It is just that I am a

Magnet
for
Disaster.

Only now I think about it, maybe it is all Aunt Deedee's fault. Because she is the one who bought the real leather briefcase in the first place.

Penny Dreadful's
Show-and-Tell

There are absolutely lots of people in my class

that are completely and very **ANNOYING**, e.g.

1. Henry Potts, who is always throwing things like rubbers and rulers.

2. Brady O'Grady, who is also always throwing things like rubbers and rulers and sometimes Henry Potts.

3. Alexander Pringle, who is mostly eating sandwiches when he should not be eating sandwiches.

4. Luke Bruce, who is often putting things up his nose, e.g. a baked bean and a hairclip and once a plastic dolphin (but it got stuck and he had to go to Mr. Schumann to get it pulled out with some pliers).

But the **BIGGEST ANNOYER** is Bridget Grimes, who is top of our class and Mr. Schumann's favourite and is utterly a big show-off, e.g. she has hair that is down to her waist and she is always swishing it and saying, "My hair is down to my waist, Penelope Jones, and your hair is tangled with glue in it", which is true but is definitely showing off.

Anyway, she is showing off doubly this week because she has got a bit of the moon in a glass box and it cost £100 and she has brought it in for show-and-tell and everyone goes "oooh" and "ahh", and Miss Patterson, who is our teacher, and who is tall and thin like a beanpole, says it

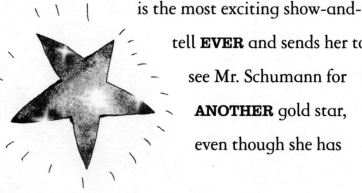

is the most exciting show-and-tell **EVER** and sends her to see Mr. Schumann for **ANOTHER** gold star, even though she has already got five gold stars for her show-and-tell objects, which were:

a. A roman coin

2. A piece of amber with a dead fly trapped in it

3. A hummingbird moth chrysalis

4. A stamp of Queen Victoria

e) Her penfriend Inka who is from Finland

I have got **NO** gold stars, even though today I have brought in a digestive that had no chocolate on it even though it came out of a chocolate digestive packet, and before that:

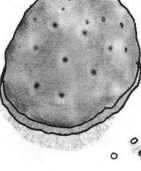

1. A dead wasp

b) A bent 2p coin

3. Magic beans, which Miss Patterson said were not magic they were just runner beans, only I said how did she know, so we planted them, and it turned out Miss Patterson was wrong because they were not runner beans, but also I was wrong because they were French beans, which are not magic, just foreign.

iv) Barry, who is Gran's cat, and who mostly does **NOT** eat cat biscuits, and who ran up the curtain in the dinner hall and got stuck, and the fire brigade had to come and rescue him and we all got to go on the fire truck (so if you think about it I should get a gold star just for that).

Which I say to Mum when I get home, and I
also say, "Please can I have a bit of the
moon in a glass box, it is only £100."
Only she says no because I have still not paid
her back from the time I accidentally phoned
India, **OR** for the hole in the carpet where I
tried to invent stain remover, **OR** for the time
Rooney chewed a hole in Daisy's doll's house —
and anyway show-and-tell is not about
EXPENSIVE objects, it is about **INTERESTING**
ones or ones you have made **ALL ALONE AND
BY YOURSELF**. And I am just about to promise
to save up £100
by doing the
washing-up
for instance,

BIT OF
MOON
£100

when the doorbell goes and
it is Cosmo Moon Webster,
who says he has come
to cheer me up about
show-and-tell and I say
it is **IMPOSSIBLE** because
I am completely **GLOOMY**.
But Cosmo says I should
be **PLEASED** that I am
not him, as he brought
in an empty glass
jar because his mum
Sunflower (who is
actually called Barbara),
said it symbolizes **SPACE**,
only Miss Patterson did not

get the **SYMBOL** and nor did Bridget Grimes, who said it is not **SPACE** unless he got the jar out of a rocket, which he did not, he just got it out of the jam cupboard.

And I say it is true because my digestive was more **INTERESTING** than the empty jar, but it did not get a gold star and I absolutely want one to beat Bridget Grimes who is a show-off. So Cosmo says what we need is a **BRAINSTORM**, which is where we think up loads of **BRILLIANT IDEAS™** and we choose the best one and that one will be the most **INTERESTING** show-and-tell object **EVER**.

✷ ✩ ✶ ✦

So what happens is we do a list and on it are:

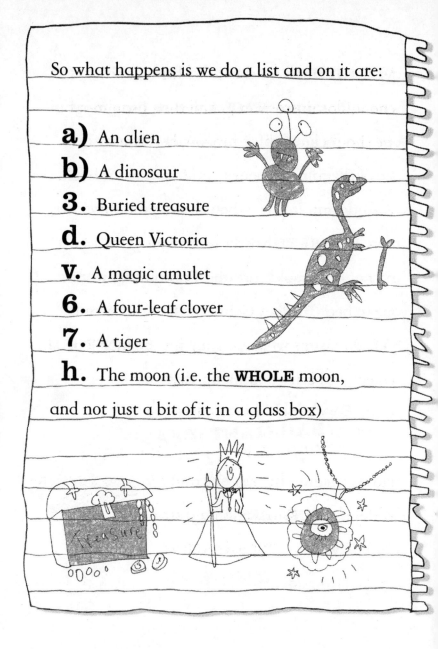

a) An alien

b) A dinosaur

3. Buried treasure

d. Queen Victoria

v. A magic amulet

6. A four-leaf clover

7. A tiger

h. The moon (i.e. the **WHOLE** moon,

and not just a bit of it in a glass box)

Which is when we decide we have done
enough brainstorming. And then I say maybe
we should cross off the moon, because we
haven't got a rocket or a pulley to get it back.
And Cosmo says we should also probably
cross off an alien too, if we cannot get to the
moon, and maybe the magic amulet, and the
tiger, and Queen Victoria, and the dinosaur.
Which means we have only got the four-leaf
clover and buried treasure ideas left for our
most **INTERESTING** object **EVER**. So I say
we should definitely get a four-leaf
clover because then it will also
bring us **LUCK** to win a gold star
as well as being **INTERESTING**,
and Cosmo agrees.

So we go **COMPLETELY QUICKLY** to the garden with a magnifying glass, and some biscuits to keep us **SUSTAINED** on our **ARDUOUS JOURNEY** (because Cosmo is very keen on **ARDUOUS JOURNEYS**, and biscuits), only when we get to the garden there has been a **COMPLETE DISASTER** because Dad has mown the lawn, i.e. there is no clover left (and no grass in places either, because the lawnmower is a bit tricky and Dad is not very good with machines),

which is not **LUCKY** at all. So then we decide to

do Plan B, which is **BURIED TREASURE**, and

we will do it in the daffodil patch, because

Barry poos in the other bits of the garden and I

do not think Miss Patterson will give me a gold

star for poo.

So we get my seaside spade, which is red and is cracked from where I tried to dig through a rock, and also a spatula from the kitchen drawer, because Daisy says we cannot borrow her spade because it is has a see-through handle with plastic fish in it which means it is special and for **SAND ONLY** and I am bound to ruin it because I am a **COMPLETE MORON**. And then

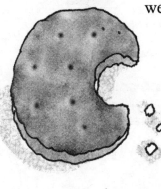

we eat our biscuits, because it has been an **ARDUOUS JOURNEY** going to the garage and the kitchen and especially to Daisy's room, because she is doubly irritating today as her friend Lucy B. Finnegan is here and they are pretending to be gymnasts.

FINALLY we start digging for buried treasure and we find some very interesting things, i.e.:

1. A rusty badge from the museum

b) A broken plate

3. A key

4. Quite a lot of daffodil bulbs

5. Another bent 2p coin

But Cosmo says mostly these are **NOT**
interesting things except for the key which
is **MYSTERIOUS** and definitely **BURIED**
TREASURE, so we show it to Mum. Only she
says there is nothing **MYSTERIOUS** about it,
it is the back door key which Dad **BURIED** in
case we were locked out, only he forgot where
he buried it so when
we **DID** get
locked out
(which was
not really my fault,
I just wanted to see
if the key fitted
through the
crack in

the pavement), we had to break in with a golf club and a hammer. **PLUS** she is not in any way pleased about the daffodil bulbs which she says need burying again **IMMEDIATELY**.

Which we do, only when we are doing the burying Cosmo stabs something metal with his spatula and he says, "Ahoy, it is buried treasure, me hearties," even though we are not being pirates we are being **ARCHAEOLOGISTS**. Plus it turns out it is not buried treasure either, it is a water pipe and water starts spurting everywhere and I say it is **LUCKY** because Mum has always wanted a water feature, only it turns out that Mum does not want a water feature that spurts in through the kitchen window.

Plus now she is **TRIPLY** not pleased because the pipes have only just been fixed after Dad unscrewed them to find Rooney the class rat.

✹ ✩ ✹ ✹

So **THEN** Gran says she has a **BRILLIANT**
and **ARCHAEOLOGICAL IDEA,** which is

that her friend Arthur Peason down the road, who

has no hair, and who is on holiday in Benidorm,

needs his vegetable patch dug over, and we can

do it for him, so it will be **INTERESTING** and

USEFUL and a **SURPRISE** all at once. And I am

very keen on being **USEFUL** and

on **SURPRISES**, only Mum is not

so sure about how **USEFUL** it

will be and about it being the

wrong sort of **SURPRISE**.

Only just then Lucy B. Finnegan does a
cartwheel into a wardrobe, which is not
USEFUL at all, but quite **SURPRISING,**

and Mum has to go upstairs to untangle her
from some coat hangers, so we go to Arthur
Peason's **COMPLETELY QUICKLY**, which is
very **ARDUOUS**, so it is lucky we have got
more biscuits.

✱ ✩ ✱ ✦

And Gran is right, it is **UTTERLY** surprising at
Arthur's, because we find a **DEAD DINOSAUR**.

What happens is I am digging with my
spade, and Cosmo is annoying some ants
with his spatula, and so far we have only got
a rusty kazoo and four ant bites, when Mrs.
Butterworth from the post office (who has a
moustache and is always saying *"I have got
my beady eye on you"*) walks past, and her
beady eye is definitely on me, because she says,

Which is possibly true, and there is nothing Mrs. Butterworth can say to that, so then she goes to be beady somewhere else. And that is when I dig something up and it is a **BONE** and underneath it are more **BONES** and I get very **EXCITED**, because not only is it

BURIED TREASURE,

it is also a

DINOSAUR,

which is two of our brainstorm things and possibly **TWO GOLD STARS**. Cosmo says he is not at all sure it is a dinosaur because it is very smallish and also has two heads, but I say **OBVIOUSLY** it is a baby two-headed dinosaur and Cosmo agrees and so we dig it all up and put it in the bucket and take it home.

And I am about to show Mum and Dad the brilliant **TWO-HEADED BURIED DINOSAUR TREASURE**, but Mum is too busy saying Dad **MUST NOT** try to fix the broken pipe, he must call **MR. HOSE**, who is the plumber, and Dad is too busy saying that he could have been a plumber if he hadn't met Mum, so there is no need to call **MR. HOSE**. And I do not want to see **MR. HOSE** at all because he is not keen on me ever since I tried to help him fix the shower, so I go to my room with the **TWO-HEADED BURIED DINOSAUR TREASURE** and Cosmo goes home with the spatula (because it is covered in ants and he is going to make an ant farm for show-and-tell, which is an **INTERESTING** object, but not as **INTERESTING** as mine).

★ ★ ✹ ✹

And **AMAZINGLY** at school the next day Miss Patterson agrees, i.e. she says the bones are possibly not dinosaur bones but they are **INFORMATIVE**, which is what show-and-tell is all about, and that I can take them to Mr. Schumann and get a gold star, which I am utterly pleased as punch about. Only then Cosmo says his ants are also **INFORMATIVE** and **EXCITING** and he takes the lid off the ant farm (which is actually a shoebox), which the ants think is very **EXCITING** and they decide to escape.

Only **LUCKILY**
I have an idea to capture
the ants, which is
ALEXANDER PRINGLE,
who is mostly eating
sandwiches in class, only this
time it will be a **GOOD THING**
because the sandwiches will
LURE the ants and they will all stick to him and
then we can **EXILE** him like Napoleon (who we
learned about in history yesterday).

Only Alexander Pringle is not so keen on being **EXILED** and the ants are not so keen on Alexander Pringle, because his sandwiches are cheese and not jam, and they are in fact more keen on Bridget Grimes, because she has brought in a meringue shaped like the Taj Mahal that she made **ALL ALONE AND BY HERSELF**. And what happens is that the ants swarm all over Bridget and one goes up her nose and she starts screaming and drops the Taj Mahal and there is meringue and ants everywhere, which is when Mr. Schumann comes in.

Mr. Schumann is quite often **SICK AND TIRED** of things, e.g. the time I proved that the most biscuits you can eat before you are sick is twenty-three. Or the time I told him Gran was dead, which was why I hadn't done my maths homework. And today he is definitely **SICK AND TIRED** and it is because of all the show-and-tell **HOO-HA**, and so he decides to **BAN** show-and-tell from now on until we can learn to bring in things that are not **ALIVE** or **FULL OF SUGAR**, e.g. a collection of thimbles or a football programme.

Only Miss Patterson says in fact Penelope Jones
has brought in something that is not **ALIVE**
or **FULL OF SUGAR**. And I say yes, it is dinosaur
bones, and Miss Patterson says no, it is not
dinosaur bones, and I say yes it is, and
Miss Patterson says no it is not, and then
Mr. Schumann decides he will be the judge of
what is a dinosaur and what isn't and he judges
and decides possibly it **IS** a dinosaur and he will
send it to the museum to check under the
microscope and in the meantime I can definitely
have a gold star. And then Mr. Eggs (who is
the caretaker and who smells of dog) comes to
clean up the meringue and the ants and we do
The Great Fire of London for the rest of the day.

✯ ✩ ✦ ✪

And I am very **EXCITED** on the way home
because of the gold star and the museum and I
absolutely burst through the door (even though
I have been told not to because once I squashed
Barry against the wall and he was not in any
way **PLEASED**), and I am about to tell everyone
that I am an **ARCHAEOLOGIST**, when I see
there is a very bald brown
man in the room
with Mum
and Dad
and Daisy
and Gran
and
he is
looking

not in any way **PLEASED** and neither are they.

And it turns out that the man is Arthur Peason,

who has got back from
Benidorm to find out that
someone has dug up George
and Mildred, who are a
dead rabbit and a dead
guinea pig, and now they
will not **REST IN PEACE**,
and nor will he until
they are
back.

And I say, It wasn't me.

And Gran says,

I told him that.

Because she is
good at keeping secrets,
especially ones that involve
me. Only it is utterly not a
secret because
Mr. Peason says
Mrs. Butterworth says she
saw me and Cosmo doing
the digging, and everyone
knows she has a beady
eye, and so I say,

Well actually, funnily enough we did not find a dead guinea pig or a dead rabbit, but we did find a dead two-headed baby dinosaur and I got a gold star for it in show-and-tell and it is being investigated at the museum under a microscope right now.

And Daisy says,

You are such a **COMPLETE MORON**, Penelope Jones.

And Dad says "Penny Dreadful" and laughs the honking goose laugh, but I do not see the funny side. And nor does Mum. And nor does Mr. Peason.

✹ ✫ ✹ ✦

And nor does Mr. Schumann, who is more **SICK AND TIRED** than **EVER** when he has to ring the museum to get George and Mildred back from under the microscope because they cannot **REST IN PEACE** and nor can Arthur Peason, and Mr. Schumann says he will possibly not **REST IN PEACE** either until I am at Broadley Comprehensive. And I say that is not for two years, four months and twenty-seven days yet. And Mr. Schumann says "Quite" and that he will have that gold star back, thank you very much, because I have proved yet again that I am utterly a menace. And I say I am not a menace, it is just that I am a

Magnet for Disaster.

But Mr. Schumann does not agree and says there is definitely no show-and-tell from now on and we can just do Romans instead.

Which is when I get my next

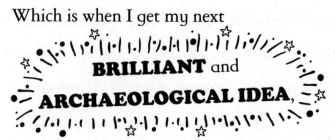

BRILLIANT and

ARCHAEOLOGICAL IDEA,

which is to find a Roman fort under our patio.

Only I cannot do it yet because my spade has

MYSTERIOUSLY disappeared and Cosmo

still has the spatula.

Our house is usually completely full of many people, i.e.:

1. Me, Penelope Jones, who is not actually dreadful, but just a **MAGNET FOR DISASTER**.

b. Daisy Jones, who is my sister, and who is not a menace either but is very **IRRITATING**.

c. Dad, who has to go to a conference on traffic lights, and is very much wishing he was in fact a deep-sea diver (which he says he could be if he hadn't met Mum).

iv) Mum, who says Dad could not be a deep-sea diver because he cannot swim underwater.

5. Barry, who is Gran's cat, and who has eaten two pieces of toast and grapefruit marmalade this morning, even though Mum says it is **CAT BISCUITS AND CAT BISCUITS ONLY**.

6 Gran, who gave Barry the toast, because she says it is her birthday and she can **DO WHAT SHE FANCIES**.

✷ ✩ ✷ ✦

Which I do not think is very fair because on
my birthday I fancied **INVENTING GOLD** and
Mum said **UNDER NO CIRCUMSTANCES**
because there is completely too much potential
for catastrophe. **BUT** it turns out that Gran
cannot **DO WHAT SHE FANCIES** either, which
is mostly eating Battenberg cake and watching
Animal SOS (which is a TV series where
animals are always nearly dying but then
they don't and it is **MIRACULOUS**), because
what happens is she accidentally trips over
my **PATENTED BURGLAR TRAP** and a bone in
her goes snap and the next thing we know she is
in hospital, where there is absolutely no cake at
all, just stew and sponge pudding.

I say it is utterly **NOT MY FAULT** because Mum said I was not to put a trap in my bedroom so I did not, I put it in the kitchen, and if you think about it, there is a **POSITIVE SIDE**, i.e. the burglar trap works and if we are ever burgled he will go snap and end up in hospital. But Mum does not see the positive side, because Dad is going to his traffic-light conference and she is going to the hospital to see Gran and there is **NO ONE** to look after me. So I say I will come to the hospital too but Mum says **UNDER NO CIRCUMSTANCES**, and she will just have to see if Lucy B. Finnegan's mum will have me as well as Daisy. Only Lucy B. Finnegan's mum says she has only just got the sticky stuff off the ceiling from last time and so she would

rather not, thank you. And
Mrs. Beasley from two doors
down would also rather not,
and neither would Arthur Peason.

And then the doorbell goes
and Mum says it had
better not be
another thing to
worry about, only it
IS another thing to
worry about, i.e. it is
Cosmo Moon Webster, who is
coming to play for the entire
and whole day because his
mum Sunflower is going to
Chipping Sodbury.

And that is when Dad has one of his

BRIGHT IDEAS™,

which is that me and Cosmo can go to Aunt

Deedee's house and be looked after by Georgia

May Morton-Jones's au pair, Lilya Bobylev.

And I can tell Mum is not in any way **KEEN**
on the **BRIGHT IDEA™**, but as Gran is
always saying **BEGGARS CAN'T BE CHOOSERS**.
So Mum puts me and Cosmo **AND** Barry in the
car (because if Barry is left on his own he gets
cross and eats his own tail) and takes us to
Aunt Deedee's house, which is only four roads
away but is very much bigger and also much
cleaner because of all the rules, e.g.:

1. No eating except at the table.

2. No plasticine or paint or glue
except at the table and only if is
covered in a plastic cloth.

C. No eating plasticine or paint
or glue.

Plus if you even **LOOK** at a glass candlestick she says, "Do not even think about it, Penelope Jones." And when we get there Lilya Bobylev is also not in any way **KEEN** on the >**BRIGHT IDEA™**,< because of the rules and the glass candlesticks and also Barry, because Aunt Deedee is **NOT A CAT PERSON** because of the fleas. But Mum says Barry does not have fleas (which is possibly a **LIE** because at that **EXACT** moment he is scratching like **MAD**), and also that Gran is Georgia May Morton-Jones's gran too and so it is **ONLY FAIR**, and then she drives off **COMPLETELY QUICKLY** before Lilya Bobylev can even **THINK** of an answer.

I say,

Do not worry, Lilya Bobylev, I am **UTTERLY RESPONSIBLE** and good at **STICKING TO RULES** and so is Cosmo Moon Webster, and if a flea does jump off Barry we will catch it and kill it with our thumbnail — I have seen it on telly.

And anyway we are utterly **ABANDONED** and practically orphans, so Lilya Bobylev has no choice but to let us in. Only when she does she says there are a lot more rules that we have to **STICK TO**, e.g.:

d. No eating in the garden.

5. No eating the garden.

6. No using purple felt-tip pen to pretend you have a DISEASE.

(which is what I did to Georgia May Morton-Jones one time, and she got sent home from The Drabble Academy for Girls in case she was **CONTAGIOUS** and Aunt Deedee had to miss a **VITAL DEAL**, which is why she has got an au pair now).

★ ★ ★ ★

And Cosmo says, "Is 'NO FUN' on the list?"
and Lilya checks and says it is not, and Cosmo
says he was being **SARCASTIC** but Lilya does
not know what that means because she is
from Russia (which is where all au pairs are
from). And then I have my first

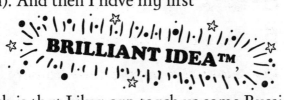

which is that Lilya can teach us some Russian,
because Aunt Deedee says it is very useful for
business brains (which is why Georgia May is
also learning Mandarin). So Lilya agrees and
says she will sing a song about a bee and a fox
and that we can join in with the chorus. Only it
is quite hard to join in because the words are

very fast and the notes are not at all normalish.
And so when Lilya is singing about the bee or
the fox (I am not sure which), Cosmo has another
BRILLIANT IDEA™, which is to do Russian
dancing, which he saw on the telly, as it has lots
of leg-kicking and arm-swooshing and is easier
than words. So me and Cosmo and Georgia
May Morton-Jones do dancing in Russian,
which is when something **UNBELIEVABLE**
happens, which is that I just **LOOK** at a glass
candlestick and it **ACTUALLY** falls off the shelf
and breaks into a gazillion pieces. And I say it
is a **MIRACLE** and Cosmo says it is not a
MIRACLE, it is because I did not just **LOOK**,
I also **SWOOSHED** it with my arm. And Lilya
also says it is not a **MIRACLE**, it is a **MESS**,

and that Georgia May Morton-Jones must **NOT TOUCH THE GLASS** because her fingers are important (because Mr. Nakamura says she shows potential on the violin) and in fact it would be a good idea if we watched television instead.

I say we can watch *Animal SOS* and then tell Gran all about it when she gets home in case she has missed it in hospital, because they do not have television, they only have romantic novels and dominoes.

Only Georgia May says she is only allowed to watch the Maths Channel, but I say if it is the Maths Channel then I am likely to be distracted and possibly may **LOOK** at another candlestick, and Lilya Bobylev thinks this is possibly true, and so we watch *Animal SOS*.

And this week the animal that almost nearly dies but then **MIRACULOUSLY** does not is a Labrador called Hoskins. What happens is that he is in a **TERRIBLE ACCIDENT** with his owner, Mr. Ernest Lemming, and they are both all broken like the candlestick and Mr. Ernest Lemming is in a coma, which is like being asleep but for at least three days (which is longer even than Cosmo who once slept for fifteen hours, which I said was a record but we checked with Mr. Schumann and it is not). But the vets on *Animal SOS* make Hoskins better by giving him some metal in his leg and a collar like a giant fan and then they take him to see Mr. Ernest Lemming, who is still in the coma, and Mr. Ernest Lemming actually **WAKES UP**.

And the presenter (who is called Griff Hunt) says "That *is* the power of pets", which is what he says every week, but this week he says it a little bit shoutier. And that is when I have my next **BRILLIANT IDEA™**, which is to take Barry to the hospital to see Gran so she can be revived by the **POWER OF PETS**.

★ ★ ★ ★

AMAZINGLY Lilya Bobylev says we can go and visit because that way the house will not get broken any more, only we **CANNOT** take Barry but we can take a Battenberg cake. Only I do

not think Battenberg cake has as much **POWER**
and so Gran will not be as **REVIVED**. And also
Cosmo says that Barry cannot be left alone
because he will eat himself and also what if a
flea jumps off him? So in the end we take him,
but Lilya says he has to go inside a bag with the
Battenberg cake, which I do not think is a good
idea because Barry once ate a whole Battenberg
cake except for the marzipan, which **AMAZINGLY**

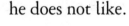 he does not like.

But I do not say anything because I want to get to the hospital super-quickly to revive Gran. Which we do because Lilya Bobylev gets to drive Aunt Deedee's car, which is "a *hideous gas-guzzling tank*" according to Mum, but "*excellent and enormous*" according to me and Cosmo. And the whole way we are singing the song about the bee and the fox in Russian like **MAD**, because by now we have all heard it quite a lot of times and so even I know some words, which are "*lisa*", which is "fox", and "*pchela*", which is "bee" – or possibly the other way round. But I don't think it matters unless the bee eats the fox, which would be impossible.

115

The only person who is not singing is Barry and
I think it is because he does not know the words,
but it turns out it is because he **IS** eating the cake.
But luckily he has only eaten the pink squares,
so I scrape off the hair and save the yellow squares
and the marzipan for Gran, who will not mind
because she is always sharing with Barry anyway,
plus he is probably very hungry on his **ARDUOUS
JOURNEY**. And then Cosmo says he is possibly
very hungry too because of the **ARDUOUS
JOURNEY** and so am I, so we decide to eat the
yellow squares and save the marzipan
for Gran, which she says is the
best bit anyway. And by
then we are at the
hospital.

Only then we realize we have **COMPLETELY** no idea which ward Gran is on and so Lilya Bobylev goes to a lady behind a desk who has glasses that make her look like an owl and asks for Granny Jones. Only the owl lady says Granny Jones is not an **ACTUAL** name and we will have to do better than that.

Except that Lilya does not know Granny's actual name and nor do I and nor does Cosmo. But Georgia May Morton-Jones says it is Norma Jean, and she goes to The Drabble Academy for Girls and so is almost often right, and this time she **IS** right because the owl lady says Norma Jean Jones is on Fothergill Ward, which is on the seventh floor. And Cosmo gets very excited about that because it means there will be a lift and he is very **KEEN** on lifts, especially on getting trapped in one and saving all the mortals who are **PANICKING** and **WAITING TO DIE**. But disappointingly the lift does not get stuck, although Barry does some panicking (even though he is not a mortal, he is a cat) and starts miaowing very loudly.

And then Georgia
May says it is very
OBVIOUS that Barry
is in the bag with the
marzipan and we
will be arrested and
sent to prison by the
hospital police. So
then I have my next
BRILLIANT IDEA™,
which is to sing the
song about the bee
and the fox in Russian
VERY LOUDLY
and **LOUDER THAN
BARRY**. So we do,

and we are still singing it when we get to
Fothergill Ward, where there is **ANOTHER** lady
behind a desk, only this one does not look like
an owl, this one looks very much like Mrs.
Butterworth from the post office, i.e. she has a
moustache, and not a beady eye but a beady
EAR, because she says,

Stop that infernal racket now, this is a hospital not a Variety Show.

ROTA

Sister Goggins

So I do stop, only then Barry is miaowing like **MAD** and so Cosmo has to pretend he is keen on being a cat. And then the beady ear lady tells him to stop **THAT** infernal racket, so he does and **AMAZINGLY** so does Barry. But it is not because of the beady ear lady it is because he is absolutely **NOT IN THE BAG**.

Which is when Georgia May Morton-Jones starts to cry, which is a **BIG MISTAKE**. Because the beady ear lady says, "What **NOW**?"

And Lilya Bobylev says it is because of Norma Jean Jones, and Georgia May says it is **NOT** because of Norma Jean Jones, it is because we have lost Barry and will be arrested by the hospital police and put in prison. And then the beady ear lady says,

And who, exactly, is Barry?

And I say,

He is our uncle.

Which is only **HALF** a lie because Gran says Barry is like a son to her, which would mean he is Dad's brother, i.e. my uncle. And the beady ear lady stops being so beady and cross and says, "Don't worry, he can't have got far," and she is **RIGHT** because at that **EXACT MOMENT** Barry runs across the floor into a cupboard

and Georgia May Morton-Jones sobs, "Barry".
Only then the beady ear lady, who is actually
called Sister Goggins and I know that because
it is on a black badge on her uniform, actually
DOES have a beady eye because she sees Barry
and makes a racket which is very **INFERNAL**.
And then **AMAZINGLY** Mum appears and also
makes a racket which is quite infernalish and is
mostly involving, "Penelope Jones, I said
UNDER NO CIRCUMSTANCES were you to
come here because there is
too much potential for
catastrophe," and I say
it is not a catastrophe
and Cosmo says it is
a **CAT**astrophe.

And then everyone is confused for a bit, but not for long because there is a big crash and some more infernal racket and then the **CAT**astrophe, i.e. Barry, who is not in any way pleased, runs out of the cupboard and towards the ill people, followed by Sister Goggins and Lilya Bobylev and Georgia May Morton-Jones and me and Mum and Cosmo.

And I say it is impressive that he is running
COMPLETELY QUICKLY because usually he is
on the sofa watching television and not even
moving a **WHISKER**. Only Sister Goggins is not
so **IMPRESSED** because she says he is possibly
killing everyone with his cat diseases.

Only when we get to the ill people they are utterly **NOT** killed by cat disease but are **REVIVED**, i.e. Gran says she feels better already just to see Barry and so does Mrs. Bickerstaff, who has a gammy eye, and so does Mrs. Goldenberg, who has a sore knee. And I say,

THAT IS THE POWER OF PETS.

Only Sister Goggins is not so convinced of the **POWER** and puts Barry inside a cardboard box with holes in it, and tapes the top up just to be sure.

And then Lilya Bobylev says she had better take Georgia May Morton-Jones home before Aunt Deedee sacks her, and Mum says she had better take me and Cosmo and Barry home because I have done enough damage for one day.

And Sister Goggins says she
hopes I will be punished,
which I do not think is
very **SISTERLY** (only I
do not say it, not even
quietly, because of the
beady ear).

And when I get home **I AM** punished and Daisy says I am a **COMPLETE MORON** and Dad does the honking goose laugh. But I do not mind because Gran gets home the next day and says she is completely **REVIVED** and that it is **ALL MY FAULT**, thanks to bringing Barry in the Battenberg bag. And for once I do not argue.

The End

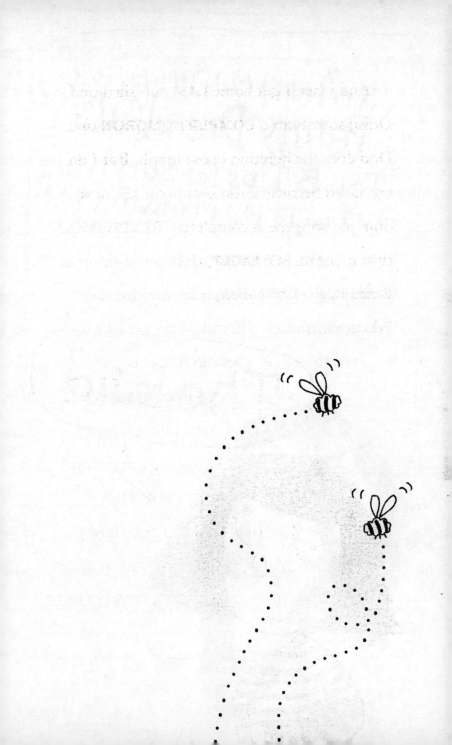

Penny Dreadful's Top 5 Tips for Survival

Sometimes it is very **ARDUOUS** being a

MAGNET FOR DISASTER. Especially if

you are extra specially magnetic, i.e. like me.

But even though it is **ARDUOUS**, it is also

very **INFORMATIVE**,

i.e. I have learned

some important

TOP TIPS

about how to

avoid complete

CATASTROPHE.

Number 1

Get a DISGUISE

It is completely
important not to
look like me, i.e.
Penelope Jones,
when I am being
very magnetic,
e.g. accidentally
knocking over a teetering pile of envelopes
in the post office. So sometimes I dress up as
Cosmo, i.e. in a Jedi outfit and wellies, because
it completely confuses Mrs. Butterworth's
beady eye and however hard she **RACKS**
her brain she is **FLUMMOXED** as to who to
shout at.

Another good disguise is dressing up as a burglar, because burglars wear balaclavas which **COMPLETELY** cover up their face.

Although it is possible you would get shouted at for being a burglar anyway.

Number 2
Collect COLLATERAL, i.e. money

Coins are **EVERYWHERE**, e.g. on the ground outside the post office, down the back of the sofa and mostly in Dad's trouser pocket.

Collect them **ALL** because you never know

when you might need them for:

1. Paying people back, e.g. your Aunt Deedee

when you have accidentally broken a glass

vase or phoned Russia for instance.

b) Buying essential supplies

like biscuits or liquorice sticks.

iii. Playing ludo, because you have

used the actual plastic counters to

flick at your mortal enemy.

Number 3
Be **PREPARED** for **EVERY EVENTUALITY**

DISASTERS are **EVERYWHERE** and you never

know when you might be super-magnetic,

so it is completely important to have a box
of useful things for **EVERY EVENTUALITY**,
i.e. anything, e.g.:

a) **COLLATERAL** (see above).

2. **A DISGUISE** (see above).

3. Biscuits (for **ARDUOUS
JOURNEYS**).

4. A bottle of washing-up liquid and a
sponge (for when you have spilled something,
or accidentally drawn some Roman soldiers
marching along the kitchen wall).

e) A torch, for when you have accidentally
blown up the hoover by trying to suck up the
washing-up liquid, and all the lights have
gone off.

Number 4

Find a TRUSTY SCAPEGOAT

This means someone else to **BLAME**, e.g. in our house everyone mostly blames me, even though it is not usually my fault, it is that I am a **MAGNET FOR DISASTER**. So I usually blame Barry the cat, because he is most often eating things that are **NOT** cat biscuits. E.g. when Daisy said, "Where is my last cherry chocolate, Penelope Jones? I **KNOW** it is you who has eaten it," I said, "But in fact perhaps it is not I, it is **BARRY**, because he is completely **KEEN** on cherries and chocolate, so ha!"

Number 5

Get a FAITHFUL FRIEND

If you are very magnetic like me, it is

COMPLETELY important to have a faithful

friend, which is not the same thing as a

scapegoat, and is also not the same as a dog,

(especially not one that isn't yours but which

you have found outside the post office only it

is not lost at all) but e.g. Cosmo Moon Webster.

Because faithful friends will always stand up

for you, even when you have accidentally

exploded custard in their microwave,

and even if they are a boy

and exactly a week

older than you.

My
Faithful Friend

Joanna Nadin

wrote this book —
and lots of others
like it. She is small,
funny, clever,
sneaky and musical.

Before she became a writer, she wanted to be a
champion ballroom dancer or a jockey, but she
was actually a lifeguard at a swimming pool,
a radio newsreader, a cleaner in an old people's
home, and a juggler. She likes Marmite on toast
for mains breakfast, and jam on toast for
pudding. Her perfect day would involve baking,
surfing, sitting in cafes in Paris, and playing
with her daughter — who reminds her
a lot of Penny Dreadful…

Jess Mikhail

illustrated this book. She loves creating funny characters with bright colours and fancy patterns to make people smile.

Her favourite place is her tiny home, where she lives with her tiny dog and spends lots of time drawing, scanning, scribbling, printing, stamping, and sometimes using her scary computer. She loves to rummage through a good car boot sale

or a charity shop to find weird and wonderful things. A perfect day for her would have to involve a sunny beach and large amounts of curry and ice cream (not together).

For Josef and Lily,
who are a little bit Cosmoish,
and totally skill because of it.

First published in the UK in 2011 by Usborne Publishing Ltd., Usborne House,
83-85 Saffron Hill, London EC1N 8RT, England. www.usborne.com

Copyright © Joanna Nadin, 2011
Illustrations copyright © Usborne Publishing Ltd., 2011

A CIP catalogue record for this book is available from the British Library.

JFMAMJ ASOND/11

ISBN 9781409536079 00113/1
Printed in Reading, Berkshire, UK.